THE CASE OF THE
Fixed Election

THE CASE OF THE
Fixed Election

Marilyn Singer

illustrations by Richard Williams

HARPER & ROW, PUBLISHERS

The Case of the Fixed Election

1 2 3 4 5 6 7 8 9 10

First Edition

Library of Congress Cataloging-in-Publication Data
Singer, Marilyn.
  The case of the fixed election / by Marilyn Singer ; illustrated
by Richard Williams.
      p.   cm.—(A Sam and Dave mystery story)
  Summary: Twin detectives Dave and Sam Bean are up to their necks
in trouble when they become enmeshed in the dirtiest
election their school has ever seen.
  ISBN 0-06-025844-6 : $. ISBN 0-06-025845-4 (lib. bdg.) : $
  [1. Politics, Practical—. 2. Elections—Fiction.
3. Schools—Fiction. 4. Twins—Fiction. 5. Mystery and detective
stories.] I. Williams, Richard, ill. II. Title. III. Series.
PZ7.S6172Caq 1989   88-21178
[Fic]—dc19   CIP
                                                AC

Acknowledgments
Thanks to Steve Aronson, Anne Gwaltney, Jay Kerig,
Oak Kerig, Leslie Kimmelman, Donn Livingston,
Andrew Ottiger, and Karl Ottiger

THE CASE OF THE
Fixed Election

1

BRAD COHEN IS NOT A CLONE
HE'S GOT A BRAIN THAT'S ALL HIS OWN
VOTE COHEN FOR PRESIDENT

read the sign. A chunky, dark-haired boy was tacking it on the bulletin board near the school cafeteria.

A short, wiry girl in a yellow dress rushed up to the board and planted another sign squarely next to his. This one said:

ELECT CORKY LEMON FOR PRESIDENT
BECAUSE THIS LEMON IS A **PEACH**

The two sign posters took a moment to admire their handiwork. Then they turned and glared at each other.

"You don't have a chance, Lemon," sneered the boy.

"That's what you think, Cohen," answered

Corky. With a toss of her head, she marched past him.

Brad thumbed his nose at her and galumphed off in the opposite direction.

"Those two don't like each other very much," said Dave Bean to his twin brother, Sam.

Sam wasn't really thinking about what Brad and Corky thought of each other. Instead, he was marveling at how fast they (and their campaign managers) had worked. Their signs were all over the school already. Dave was running for Student Council president too, and Sam was his campaign manager. But not only hadn't they put up his signs, they hadn't even made them yet. They couldn't seem to come up with a good slogan. Before Sam had a chance to say anything, Jack Dodge, the only candidate for vice president, said in his nasal voice, "As a reliable witness to the preceding incident, I'll corroborate that."

Sam looked at him blankly. Jack's father was a lawyer, and Jack was always using big legal words and phrases hardly anybody understood. It was annoying. Jack was annoying. But when it came to "good causes," he was also the hardest-working kid in the school. Right now he had a petition he wanted Sam and Dave to sign. It was about saving some big trees near the school that a developer wanted to cut down. Sam and Dave read the petition. While they were signing it, Jack asked, "Where are your posters, Dave?"

"We'll be putting them up soon," Dave said, thinking that that had better be true. "What do we have so far, sloganwise?" he whispered to Sam as Jack dashed over to their gym teacher to get his signature on the petition.

Sam pulled out his notebook and read, " 'Dave Bean—he's keen'; 'Dave Bean is no beanbag'; 'Vote for Dave—one of the best human Beans around.' "

"Ugh, ugh, and ugh," said Dave.

"Yeah." Sam nodded.

Jack rejoined them. "Well, I want to wish you good luck on your campaign, Dave. You'll be getting my vote. It's no mystery you're the best candidate for the job." He patted Dave on the back and charged off into the cafeteria, waving his petition like a flag.

Sam and Dave looked at each other.

"It's no mystery . . ." Dave began.

"You're the best candidate for the job," finished Sam.

"Not a bad slogan, with a few changes . . ."

". . . for a famous detective."

Sam and Dave slapped five. "Thanks, Jack," they chorused to the empty hall. Then, laughing, they went into the cafeteria to eat lunch.

That evening they worked on the posters. Sam picked out the colors; Dave came up with the design; and they both did the lettering.

"These look great," Dave said when they finished. "Let's go in early tomorrow to put them up."

"Yeah," agreed Sam, wondering if Brad and Corky had left them any wall space. Brad, Corky, and Dave, all of them running for president and all of them wanting to win. Sam thought his brother had a good chance, but he wasn't a shoo-in. Brad was pretty popular, and Corky had a lot of friends too. It was going to be a tight race.

"I hope it'll be a clean one," Dave said.

"What?" Sam looked up at him.

"The election. With the way Brad and Corky are acting, I hope there won't be any dirty tricks."

"Do you think there will be?" Sam asked.

Dave hesitated a moment, then shook his head. "No," he said. He repeated it firmly. "No."

But Sam didn't think he looked so sure about it.

"Spudnuts," said Rita O'Toole.

Sam groaned. Rita didn't notice. Dave did. He turned to Sam and gave him a sideways grin.

"That's what's going to win this election—

Spudnuts," continued the tall, thin, super-smart redhead. Sam and Dave had become friends with Rita when they'd helped find her missing brother, Leroy. "You can be for Spudnuts, like Corky and her gang. Or against Spudnuts, like Brad and his. But you can't be middle of the road. Don't you agree, Sam . . . Sam, are you okay? You look a little green."

Sam nodded. He agreed with Rita—and he was green. The mention of Spudnuts did that to him. For years, Sam and his classmates had had to sell the potato-flour doughnuts to raise money for the school treasury. Some kids liked doing it—they felt that Spudnuts were a school tradition. But other kids (and not only kids) were sick of the things. Last year, when Sam had tried to sell them, his neighbors had greeted him with "Not Spudnuts again." He got stuck having to buy six dozen himself. His parents wouldn't let him have any dessert until he'd eaten every last Spudnut. Dave helped out some, but Sam still had to dispose of most of them. This year he planned to be sick on the day the Spudnuts were distributed. But Dave's running for president changed Sam's plans.

"I'm okay," he told Rita.

She shrugged and turned back to Dave. "So, where do you stand on the Spudnuts issue?" she asked, as they walked down the hall toward the school exit, passing Jack Dodge on the way. He was busy setting up a booth to collect toys for needy children. He waved at them.

"Oh, I would have to say I'm anti-Spudnut," Dave said, clapping Sam on the shoulder and grinning at him again. Then, more seriously, he added, "I think we should sell pumpkins at the Fall Fair instead."

"Good idea," Rita approved. "Very innovative." She used almost as many big words as Jack, except she wasn't obnoxious about it. "Make sure you include that in your speech tomorrow at Meet-The-Candidates Day."

"I will," said Dave.

Outside the school, it looked as if Meet-The-Candidates Day was already happening. Brad Cohen was greeting every departing student. "Hi. How are you? I'm your candidate for president," he said, shaking hands just the way Congressman Clayton had done at the shopping mall the day before, and flashing a big toothy grin.

"Hey, Brad," a kid yelled out. "You running for Student Council president or for Mr. Brush-After-Every-Meal?"

Brad's smile began to fade. Dan Lipsky, his campaign manager, called out, "Hey, Lawson, is that you?"

"Yeah," the kid answered.

"How'd you do yesterday?"

"We won, twenty-one to fourteen."

"Way to go!" Dan exclaimed. "Like Brad said to me just this morning, you guys are the best football team we've ever had."

"All right!" Lawson responded, pumping his fist in the air. Several of his teammates echoed him.

Sam shook his head. Slick. Very slick, he thought. Dan had probably just gotten eleven votes for Brad. But Sam wasn't certain how much he admired the way Dan had done it. It seemed so phony. He frowned.

"That's funny," Dave said dryly. "I heard Dan tell Brad in gym that the football team stinks, and Brad agreed."

Sam's frown widened. Dan sure *was* a phony. Sam was about to comment on that to Dave and Rita when something clipped him on the arm and pinged at his feet. He picked it up. It was a black metal button with a bright-yellow lemon on it.

"Whoops! Sorry about that. It just flew out of my hand," Corky said. She had a basketful of buttons over her arm, and today she was wearing yellow pants. She'd worn something yellow every day for a week. "You can keep it if you want, Dave."

"Sam," he replied. Corky's voice was friendly enough, but he couldn't help wondering if she'd hit him with the button accidentally or on purpose.

"Whoops again."

9

"No, he can't keep it," said Missy Mason, her campaign manager, snatching the button out of his hand. "He'll just throw it away, and they're too expensive to waste."

"Hey, can I have one of those?" a girl called out to her from near where Brad and Dan were standing.

"Sure," said Missy. "Come on, Corky. You've got to meet your public." She shooed Corky toward the girl.

Corky gave Sam and Dave a glittery smile over her shoulder and walked away.

"She must've spent a bundle on those buttons," Dave said.

"Yeah," agreed Sam, thinking it was too bad they couldn't afford to make up buttons for Dave.

"Forget the buttons. Forget the football team. Stick to the issues, stick to Spudnuts and you'll . . ."

Rita's pep talk was cut off by a shriek and a sound like a splatter of raindrops on a tin roof that came from where Corky and Missy had gone.

"He pushed me! He pushed me, the creep!" Corky bellowed.

"The buttons! Watch out! You're stepping all over them," Missy shouted at the same time.

Sam, Dave, and Rita hurried down to the crowd that had gathered around the girls. Missy was kneeling on the ground, scooping up bunches of buttons that lay scattered around her. Red-faced and scowling, Corky was pointing at Brad. "He did it! He pushed me!" she accused.

"I did not!" Brad glowered.

"You did too."

"I did not!"

"Now, Corky. Brad wouldn't do that," Dan told her calmly.

"He would too. He pushed me."

"The buttons!" Missy wailed. "They're ruined." She held out a scratched and dented handful.

Corky glanced at them quickly, then back at Brad and Dan. "I'm going to get you for this," she threatened.

"Not if I get you first, Spudnutter," Brad sneered.

Some of the kids in the crowd giggled.

Corky whirled to glare at them and saw Sam and Dave. "You think it's funny, huh? Well, Bean Brothers, we'll see who has the last laugh."

Sam and Dave looked at each other with raised eyebrows. They hadn't been laughing at Corky before, and they weren't laughing now.

3

Sam was in the boys' room when he first heard the rumor. He was feeling nervous because it was Meet-The-Candidates Day and Dave would soon be making the speech they'd written the night before. Dave didn't seem to be very nervous about it, though. The butterflies always land in *my* stomach, Sam said to himself as he washed his hands.

At the sink next to his, Jack was quietly rehearsing his speech. "As your candidate for vice president, I wish to make this statement: I will perform my duties with diligence and enthusiasm. Let me direct your attention to Exhibit A— my good-citizenship award from last year . . ."

"Hey, Jack, why are you making a speech?" one of his classmates teased him. Kids were always teasing Jack. "You're the only one running for vice president. We *have* to vote for you— unfortunately."

"Yeah, and why are you running for vice president anyway?" another kid asked. "The vice president doesn't do anything unless something happens to the president. Why don't you run for president? You might get a vote or two."

Jack ignored them and went on rehearsing. Sam sighed. His speech sounded like a long one,

which meant Sam would have lots of time to get even more nervous before Dave finally made his.

Then behind him Sam heard someone say, "Did you know that her uncle makes Spudnuts? No wonder she wants us to keep selling those things. She gets money for every dozen we sell. It's called a *percentage*."

Sam turned his head quickly and recognized Tim Lawson, the football player, and one of his teammates.

"Gee, I'm not voting for her, then," the other boy said.

"Good . . . Brad Cohen's the right man for the job anyway." Lawson's voice faded away as the two boys left the room.

They're talking about Corky, Sam thought. They think she's involved in some scam. He turned to Jack to catch his reaction. But Jack wasn't listening.

Sam dried his hands swiftly and hurried out of the boys' room to the cafeteria.

"I just heard a rumor . . ." he began.

"About Corky Lemon," Dave and Rita finished simultaneously.

"You heard it too?"

"It's all over the school—that her grandfather makes Spudnuts and she gets a quarter for every dozen we sell," said Rita.

"I heard that it's her father and fifty cents," Dave put in.

Sam told his version. "Who do you think started it?" he asked.

"We were wondering the same thing. Brad, maybe. Remember what he said yesterday—'Not if I get you first.' Or it could be Dan Lipsky. Or both of them," said Dave.

"It could be Lawson. To help out Brad."

"Maybe."

"Do you think it's true?"

"I don't know. But if other kids do, Corky's campaign is in big trouble—and Corky's going to be out for revenge."

4

The auditorium was full. Dave peeked out at the buzzing students from the wings of the stage. He still wasn't very nervous about making his speech, but he was worried about what would happen when Corky gave hers. The rumor had flown around the school faster than the Concorde, and Dave could sense the three hundred kids out front eagerly awaiting her appearance. He was desperately hoping that what he was afraid would happen wouldn't.

He glanced over at Corky. She was standing

15

off to the side. Her yellow blouse against the brown-painted wall made Dave think of butter on toast. She must've heard the rumor by now, he thought. She must be melting. But he couldn't tell from her blank face, and that made him even more concerned.

Slouched in a chair, out of her view, Brad was also watching Corky. He felt Dave's eyes on him and looked his way. He gave the kind of curt nod a boxer would give to an opponent and went back to watching Corky.

Then Dr. Barron, the principal, appeared. "Okay. Time to begin," she said, motioning to the stage.

The candidates filed out. The buzzing swelled to a dull roar. Dave stared out into the audience, searching for Sam. He found him in the second row, with Rita sitting next to him. He looks more scared than I am, Dave thought affectionately. He was right. The butterflies in Sam's stomach had grown as big as bats. But Sam gave him a smile and held up a pair of crossed fingers. Rita did the same, then stuck her fingers under her nose to fight back a sneeze.

Dr. Barron crossed the stage to the microphone and silenced everyone. She gave a short speech about democracy and then introduced the candidates.

The buzzing started up again as the would-be treasurers and secretaries spoke, and it nearly

16

drowned out Jack Dodge, whose speech was just as long and dull as Sam had feared it would be. Dave tried to listen with interest, but even he had to fight to keep from fidgeting.

"Can it, Jack," Tim Lawson called out.

"Quiet!" ordered one of the teachers.

"But he's boring!" said someone else. "And he sounds like he's talking through his nose."

This time it was Dr. Barron who demanded silence and everybody settled down again.

But not for long. The presidential candidates were up next. Dave began to pant a little, the way he always did just before his entrance in a play. And again, just like always, he took a deep breath and told himself to relax. Then he went to the mike. "My name is Dave Bean," he began, speaking clearly and easily. "I'd like to promise you longer lunch breaks, less homework, and better food in the cafeteria. But I can't."

The audience laughed. Sam, who'd helped write the speech, laughed too and began to settle down. Rita couldn't laugh. She was sneezing too hard.

"So here's what I can promise," Dave continued, laying out his platform. He talked about improving after-school activities, planning more dances, and sponsoring a foreign exchange student. When he got to his idea of selling pumpkins at the Fall Fair to raise money, the audience applauded enthusiastically. He caught Sam's eye again and grinned. Sam grinned back and gave him a thumbs up sign. Feeling pretty good, Dave finished his speech and returned to his seat.

It was Brad's turn next. "Nice *try*," he said, emphasizing the second word.

"Thanks a lot," Dave answered dryly.

Brad strode across the stage and grabbed the mike like a rock singer. His voice boomed across the big room. "I'm Brad Cohen, and if I'm elected I promise you this: No More Spudnuts!"

A cheer went up from the audience.

"We're going to sell something people will really buy. Not potato doughnuts." He looked at Corky. "Not pumpkins." He turned to Dave. "We're gonna sell . . ." He paused dramatically, staring out at the crowd. "Sticky Babies."

"Hooray!" "Yeah!" The cheers were louder.

Dave looked at Sam and gave a slight shrug. He hadn't thought about selling candy. Some parents didn't approve of it. But the kids sure liked the idea.

Brad didn't have much else to add to his speech, but the audience didn't seem to care. They were all excited now. And they were ready for Corky.

With a smile almost as big and bright as Brad's, Corky seemed ready for them. There was a sudden silence as she took her place at the mike. Dave found himself holding his breath. He let it out slowly as she began, "Fellow students, I'm Corky Lemon and I . . ."

That was as far as she got before the chant

began. "Spudnutter, Spudnutter, Spudnutter," it went, low, rumbling, and nasty. "Spudnutter, Spudnutter."

Dave craned his neck to see who and where it was coming from, but he couldn't tell. He saw Sam glancing around too and Rita trying to as well, but sneezing instead.

Corky's smile wavered, but she fixed it back in place. "I . . . I'm running for Student Council president, and if I'm elected . . ."

"Spudnutter, Spudnutter, Spudnutter."

Missy Mason jumped up from the front row and glared at everyone.

"I promise . . . I promise to put more mirrors in the girls' room and . . . and . . ."

"Spudnutter, SPUDNUTTER!"

"Silence!" ordered Dr. Barron.

"Stop it!" yelled Missy. "Stop it! There's nothing wrong with Spudnuts. They're a school tradition. We make a lot of money from them."

"Yeah—and so does Corky!" Tim Lawson hollered.

"Liar! Who said that?" Corky demanded, her smile gone, her voice high and shrill. "Whoever did is a liar!"

"Yeah? And I suppose it's also a lie that your *uncle* makes Spudnuts?"

Corky turned pale. She stood still, her mouth opening and closing. Then, with a cry, she ran off the stage. Missy ran after her.

19

The audience laughed and hooted.

Dave shook his head in disgust.

"Well, scratch one opponent." Brad smirked.

"Did you start that rumor?" Dave asked him, more sharply than he'd intended.

"Me? No."

"Do you know who did?"

"No. But whoever did, did us both a favor. If I were you, Mr. Detective, I'd leave this one alone."

Dave didn't answer him. He just rose slowly and walked off the stage.

5

Rita felt terrible. Her head ached. Her throat was sore. Her nose was so stuffed she wouldn't have been able to smell her brother's dirty socks even if he held them right under her nostrils. She knew she was too sick to go to school, but she was going anyway. It was Election Day, and Rita had to go vote for Dave. After what had happened yesterday, Rita thought that Corky probably didn't have much of a chance of winning anymore. But Brad, if anything, had gained more popularity—so Dave needed every vote he could get. With a groan, Rita pushed off her blankets, got up, and began to get dressed.

Even though the day was warm and she had on a sweater and a jacket, she felt chilly and dizzy by the time she reached school. The front yard was nearly deserted. Great. I'm late as well as sick, she thought grumpily, trying to walk faster. A light breeze sprang up, swirling some stray papers off the ground and making her shiver. One sheet slapped on to her leg. She peeled it off and was about to crumple it when she noticed it was scrawled all over with signatures. One signature to be exact: Dave Bean's. Rita stared at the paper, puzzled. Maybe Dave had been doodling, but where did that paper come from? The sheet of printed stationery didn't resemble anything she'd ever seen Dave write on. One corner was torn, but she could still read some of the letters on it:

esk of

ge, Esq.

They didn't mean anything to her. I'll show this to Dave and Sam, she thought, slipping the paper into her notebook. Another wave of dizziness hit her and she shivered again.

She entered the building and wobbled down the hall to her classroom. Everyone was already seated. Ms. Corfein was taking attendance. On her desk was a big ballot box and next to it a crisp little pile of blank pieces of paper.

"Oh, Rita. You are here," the teacher said. "Take your seat now. We're going to have a surprise spelling test."

But Rita didn't take her seat. "Uh, Ms. Corfein," she said. "Do you mind if I vote first?"

Ms. Corfein gave her a strange look. "We're all going to vote after the spelling test."

"Uh . . . please can I vote now?" Rita begged, swaying slightly by the teacher's desk.

"Is something the matter?"

"I . . .uh . . . I think I'd concentrate better on the test if I voted first."

"I'm sure you'll concentrate just fine right now, Rita. You're our best speller."

Then Rita did something she'd never normally do. She snatched a piece of paper and a pen off Ms. Corfein's desk, quickly wrote "Dave Bean—President," plus the names of the other candidates she was voting for, and dropped it in the ballot box.

"Rita!" exclaimed Ms. Corfein, shocked.

Rita turned to Dave, gave him a brief smile, and fell in a dead faint on the floor.

6

For the twentieth time that morning, Sam and Dave exchanged worried looks. There was plenty for them to worry about. What was wrong with

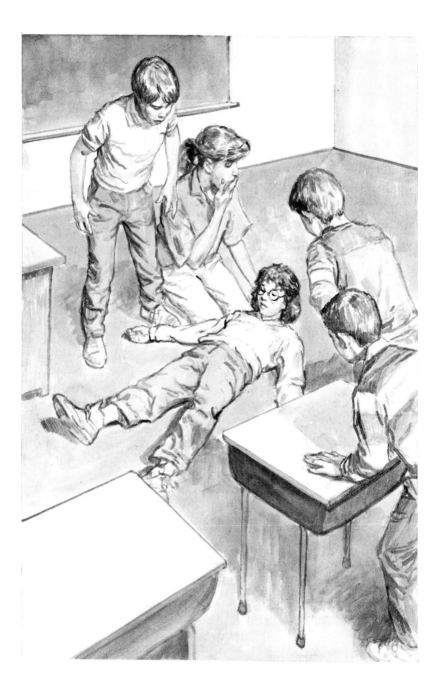

Rita? Who had won the election? What was going to happen next? Would Corky take some kind of revenge if she lost? The day was dragging on without any of their questions being answered.

Then, the phone in their classroom rang. Ms. Corfein answered it. "Yes? Yes? Yes," she said. She hung up and told the class that Rita had a bad case of the flu. "She needs plenty of rest, but she'll be fine."

Sam and Dave turned to each other once more and sighed with relief.

"Now, Sam, you're the class monitor," said Ms. Corfein. "Will you please take the ballot box to Dr. Barron's office so she can count the votes."

"It's about time," Dave whispered.

Sam grinned. Dave hardly ever expressed his impatience. "You can say that again," he whispered back.

Sam picked up the small box from Ms. Corfein's desk and, forcing himself not to run, loped out of the room.

It didn't take him much time to reach the principal's office, but there was already a line of kids ahead of him, each bearing a ballot box.

"Good heavens. What are all of you doing here?" Dr. Barron's secretary exclaimed, waving a phone in one hand and a bunch of folders in the other. Her name was Ms. Lutz, but everyone called her Ms. Clutz. With good reason.

"It's Election Day. We've got the votes for the Student Council officers," a girl explained.

"Oh yes, that's right. That's right. Well, just dump them in there, will you?" Ms. Lutz pointed with the folders to a large box by the windowsill. The folders slid out of her hand and scattered all over the floor. "Oh, good grief!" She stooped down to pick them up and the phone popped out of her other hand, clattering against a vase, which didn't break, but tipped over and rolled to the floor, dousing the folders with water, leaves, and flower petals.

"Clutz," someone murmured. There were stifled giggles. Sam had to bite his lip to keep from laughing.

"Oh, good night!" cried Ms. Lutz. She bent to retrieve the vase and the folders and a small stream of water dribbled from the desk onto her head.

There were more giggles, until the secretary rose and gave everyone a dirty look. "I'm going to get some paper towels. If anybody touches anything in this room other than that box, he or she will have a date with Dr. Barron!" She marched out—and everyone roared with laughter.

She still hadn't returned by the time Sam, hiccuping from the giggles, had shaken the last ballot out of his box. He turned around to go and saw Dan Lipsky sitting there watching him.

"Well, you're sure one talented guy—office

monitor, campaign manager, and detective," Dan said, slick as usual.

What's he bothering to compliment me for? Sam wondered. The votes are already in and he knows I wouldn't vote for Brad anyway. But Sam said thanks, asked politely, "Are you an office monitor too?" and immediately felt dumb. Of course Dan wasn't. He didn't have a ballot box with him. Any decent detective could see that.

But Dan answered, with a smile, "No. I'm here to see . . . Ms. Lutz." He hesitated only slightly, but Sam caught it.

"Ms. Lutz?"

"That's right, Ms. Lutz," Dan said, smoothly this time. "I've got to get permission to make a phone call."

"Oh."

"Well, I guess you've got to get back to class."

Sam paused. The office was empty now except for the two of them, and Dan sounded like he was eager for Sam to go, which made him feel like he should stick around. But Ms. Corfein *was* waiting for Sam to return so everyone could go to lunch. "Yes, I do," he said reluctantly. Slowly he walked out and nearly collided with Jack Dodge.

"Sam! Just the person I've been wanting to see," Jack said cheerfully, keeping pace with him. "You know the Toy Drive? We collect toys to give to needy children. I need a couple more volunteers to run it. I've got Brad and Missy and Judy, and I'd like to have you. All you have to do is watch the kids drop the toys in the bin, then lock up and hand the key to Ms. Lutz. You'll pick up the key from her or from the person working the booth before you. I'll put you down for the second half of lunch period, Monday through Friday, okay?"

"All right," Sam agreed. As Jack turned and bustled down the hall, past the principal's office and around the corner, Sam groaned. The second half of lunch period? Monday through Friday? What had he gotten himself into this time? That Jack. He got you to say yes before you knew what you were saying yes to. But at least it was for a good cause.

Shaking his head, Sam hurried toward his classroom. Just as he reached the end of the corridor, he heard faint footsteps behind him. He spun around and saw a girl disappearing into Dr. Barron's office. He couldn't make out her face, but he got a clear view of her skirt. It was bright, bright yellow.

7

Dong, ding, dong! chimed the loudspeaker on the cafeteria wall. "Attention, attention. This is Dr. Barron."

Dave laid down the juice container he'd just raised. "Here it comes," he said.

Sam nodded. He suddenly wanted to grab his brother's hand and hold it the way he used to when they were little. Instead, he did a brief drum roll on the table.

"All the votes for Student Council officers have been counted," Dr. Barron's voice continued. "Here are the results. Secretary, Karen Chen. Treasurer, Gina Escobar. Vice president, Jack Dodge. President . . . Dave Bean."

Sam and Dave let out their breath together and slapped five.

Cheers and shouts of "All right!" "Way to go, Bean!" and "Congratulations, Dave!" echoed all over the cafeteria. Kids came by to pat Dave on the back and tell him they were glad he'd won. Across the room, Brad glowered and turned away. Corky was nowhere to be seen.

"How about going to Roma's after school to celebrate with a kitchen sink pizza?" Dave suggested to Sam. "My treat—after all, I couldn't have won without such a good campaign manager."

Sam didn't know whether or not that was true, but he appreciated the fact that his brother believed it. "Sounds good to me. It's too bad Rita can't join us," he said, a little shyly.

"Yeah. But we can celebrate again when she's better. Then we can have another kitchen sink, and you can treat."

Sam laughed. Dave joined in.

They were feeling really good when they went back to Ms. Corfein's class. The good feeling lasted for a solid hour until a monitor came into the classroom with a note. Ms. Corfein read it and told Sam and Dave that Dr. Barron wanted them to come to her office immediately.

"Hey, looks like the principal wants to congratulate you in person, Dave," said one of his classmates.

"Yeah, and since she can't tell who's Dave and who's Sam, she figured she'd play it safe and have you both there," said someone else.

Everyone laughed—except Sam and Dave. They couldn't begin to guess why Dr. Barron would want to see them. Dave took the pass that Ms. Corfein was holding out, and the two brothers walked side by side to the principal's office.

"I'm new to this school, but I've been a principal for fifteen years. I've seen a lot, and not much surprises me anymore. But frankly, this does—especially from two boys who don't have a blot on their records." Dr. Barron shook her head. "We might not even have discovered it if Dan Lipsky hadn't demanded a recount."

Sam said nothing. His mouth was hanging open as he stared down at the hundred and six ballots spread out on Dr. Barron's desk. They were all for Dave Bean. And they were all in Dave's handwriting.

"We didn't do this, Dr. Barron," Dave protested. "We didn't stuff the ballot box."

"Isn't this your handwriting? And isn't your brother the office monitor for your class?"

"Sam is the office monitor, but he didn't put any ballots in the box except for his own. And this . . . this *looks* like my handwriting. But it isn't."

"Can you prove that?"

"No. At least, not yet."

"Well I can give you a day or two to try. However, if you don't come up with something, I'm afraid I'll have no choice but to disqualify you as a candidate and to call for a new election between Brad and Corky."

"You . . . you can't do that, Dr. Barron," Sam blurted out. "It isn't fair!" He was angry. So angry he forgot to be the shy, quiet boy he usually was. Dave laid a hand on his shoulder, telling him to calm down.

"Is this fair?" Dr. Barron said sternly. Then, more gently, "I'm sorry, boys. It's possible that

you're telling the truth. But unless you can find something out, I have no choice." She looked at Dave. "You can return to class now."

Sam stared at the principal for a moment. His eyes stung. He was afraid he might start crying.

"Come on, Sam," Dave said, steering him out of the office.

Neither of them said anything until they reached their classroom. Then, just before they went inside, Dave broke the silence. "Well," he said. "It looks like Bean Brothers, Private Eyes, have got an interesting new set of clients—themselves."

"Dan Lipsky. He's the Number One suspect. You said he was in the office alone and that you didn't believe him when he said he was there to see Ms. Lutz. And he demanded the recount," Dave said, as he and Sam sat on the stone turtle in the playground after school.

"Corky could've done it too. I'm pretty sure I saw her go into the principal's office," said Sam. "Or it might have been someone else I didn't see."

"We've got to talk to her and Dan."

"It won't help much. Whoever forged your signature and stuffed the box isn't going to admit it."

"I know," said Dave. "But we've got to talk to them anyway."

Sam nodded. "Okay. Let's go."

They tried Dan first, because he lived nearest the school. He was perfectly willing to talk with them. But just as they'd thought, he denied any wrongdoing.

"Then why did you ask for a recount?" Dave questioned him.

"Because Brad lost. A good campaign manager always demands a recount if his candidate loses."

"What were you really doing in the principal's office?" said Sam. "You said you were waiting for Ms. Lutz—but I don't think you were telling the truth."

Dan hesitated. Dave thought he looked like he was trying to decide whether or not to lie again. "Maybe we should ask her," Dave put in.

"Okay. I'll level with you," Dan said in his best honest-guy voice. "I wasn't there to see her. I was there to see Dr. Barron. About a little trouble over a science test. My teacher seemed to think I was . . . uh . . . borrowing some of the answers. I wasn't, of course."

"Of course," muttered Sam.

Dan ignored him. "Dr. Barron believed me. You can ask her." He smiled.

Sam frowned. He knew Dr. Barron would under no circumstances talk to them about a fellow student and that Dan knew that too. He might or might not be a cheat. Just like he might or might not have stuffed the ballot box.

They left his house feeling frustrated. They became even more frustrated when they tried to talk to Corky at her home and she refused to open the door for them.

They sat on her stoop. "Well, at least we tried," said Dave, philosophically. "Anyway, Corky doesn't have much of a motive for stuffing the box. That rumor really wrecked her campaign. Disqualifying me isn't going to help her win against Brad."

"Maybe there's some other reason she did it," Sam said.

They thought a moment. Then Dave said, "That rumor. Sam, where do they make Spudnuts?"

"Out in Oakdale, I think. We can look it up in the phone book to be sure."

"Oakdale. That's not very far. We can get there and back home in time for dinner."

Sam looked at Dave in horror. "We're going to go to the Spudnuts factory?" His stomach lurched. "I'm going to be surrounded by thousands of . . . *ulp* . . . Spudnuts?"

Dave grinned at him. "Millions," he said.

There were no Spudnuts in the office, but there might as well have been. The whole place reeked of them, the odor wafting in from the nearby ovens. Wishing he had some cotton to plug up his nose, Sam tried his best not to breathe. It didn't work. He still smelled Spudnuts. He prayed that he and Dave could find out what they needed to know and get out of there soon, before his stomach embarrassed both of them.

"Hello, we'd like to talk to the owner," Dave said to the receptionist, a plump woman with a lot of frizzy hair. Her desk plate said her name was Ms. Gardella.

"Twins! How adorable!" she exclaimed. "I have twin sisters. I mean, they're not my twins—then we'd be triplets. Ha ha!"

Dave smiled politely. Sam tried to smile and burped instead.

"How do you like being twins? My sisters love it. They're always pretending they're each other to fool everybody. Do you do that?"

"Not usually."

"Once they went out on a date with one guy. . . ."

Sam smothered a groan. We're going to be here all day, he thought, as Ms. Gardella chattered on. I'll never make it. He turned pleading eyes on Dave.

Dave didn't look his way, but interrupted politely. "Excuse me, but do you think the owner would be able to see us now, Ms. Gardella?"

"Oh, no. I'm afraid not. Mr. Lamb's busy.

What do you need to see him about? Not a job, I hope. You're both a little too young."

"No, it's for . . . school."

"School, eh? Which school do you go to?"

Dave told her.

"Oh, Mr. Lamb's niece goes there."

Sam suddenly forgot about his stomach. "His niece?" he said.

Ms. Gardella looked at him. "Hey, you okay? You look a little green."

"He's fine," Dave said. "He always looks that way."

"Yeah? Is he from Vulcan? Ha ha!"

"You mentioned Mr. Lamb's niece," Dave said, bringing her back to the subject. "Who is she? We might know her."

"You might. Her name's Corky Lemon. She's a nice girl. Has a good business sense too. That's why Mr. Lamb offered her a commission to help sell Spudnuts in your school."

Dave felt Sam glance at him, but he purposely avoided returning it. He didn't want Ms. Gardella to clam up now. "Really?" he said calmly. "Did she accept?"

"As I told that other boy, I haven't the foggiest idea."

"What other boy?"

"The one who phoned a few days ago about Corky and Mr. Lamb. Said he was doing an article on her and Spudnuts for your school paper."

"You wouldn't happen to remember his name, would you, Ms. Gardella?" Dave asked.

"Why, as a matter of fact I would, because it was funny. Like I said to Corky just yesterday, it sounded like a menu."

"A menu?"

"Yes. Their names. All foods. Lamb, Lemon, and Bean. The boy's name was Dave Bean."

9

"All right, class," said Ms. Corfein. "It's time to vote."

"Again," rang out a voice from the back of the classroom.

"Hey, Sam and Dave, who are you voting for this time?" "Hey, Bean Brothers, it's no mystery who stuffed the ballot box," teased other kids.

Sam and Dave sat there quietly and took it. They knew that anything they said would only make matters worse. Two days had passed and they hadn't been able to catch the real culprit and clear their names. So Dr. Barron had reluctantly disqualified Dave. But he and Sam weren't going to give up. They knew now that Corky had a motive, as did Dan. However, Corky certainly wasn't the one who had used Dave's name to start the rumor that messed up her campaign. Had the same person started the rumor *and* stuffed the box? Sam and Dave wished they could talk to Rita. She might have some ideas. But Rita was still quite ill. Her mother wouldn't even allow her to talk on the phone. It looked as though the Bean Brothers weren't going to get any help solving this case, but solve it they had to. And soon.

"That's quite enough, class," said Ms. Corfein. She looked at Sam and Dave and shook her head.

We didn't do it, Ms. Corfein, they wanted to tell her, just as they'd told Dr. Barron. But she hadn't quite believed them. They didn't know whether or not Ms. Corfein would either—and they weren't sure they wanted to find out.

"I'm not making any allegations, Missy. I'm just attempting to find out what happened to the toys," Jack was saying patiently. "There are two missing—a stuffed bear and a truck. They were here yesterday afternoon when I locked up. Now they're gone."

"I don't know where they are," Missy said defensively. "I certainly didn't take them. Why don't you ask the other kids who ran the booth before I did?"

"I've already spoken to Judy. I'm going to talk to . . . Oh hi, Sam. You're right on time. Are you helping out too, Dave?"

41

"Helping out with what?" Dave asked. Sam had forgotten to mention to him that he'd be working at the booth. In fact, he'd forgotten that he was supposed to be at the booth, period.

"With the Toy Drive," Jack answered.

"You're going to let *them* run the booth?" said Missy.

"Everyone is innocent until proven guilty, and to my mind, it has not been proven beyond a reasonable doubt that it was Dave or Sam who stuffed the ballot box," Jack said, sounding just like his father.

Sam and Dave cast grateful looks at him. Missy frowned. "To my mind, I know a couple of rats when they wiggle their whiskers." Without glancing at either Sam or Dave, she walked away.

There was silence for a moment, then Dave said, "I'll be glad to help out."

"Good." Jack beamed.

"But what's this about missing toys?"

Jack sighed. "It appears that someone's been pilfering."

"Any idea who it is?"

Jack hesitated. "No." Then quickly, he added, "But don't worry. I'm looking into it. Now, here's the key. You know what to do, right?"

What they had to do was simple and rather boring, but Sam and Dave didn't mind. They didn't feel like being in the cafeteria when the new election results were announced. They were pretty sure who was going to win anyway—and they were right. It was Brad. They could hear the cheers for him all the way out in the hall.

"I just hope," Dave said quietly, "that he does a good job."

And *I* hope, thought Sam, feeling less gracious, that he gets impeached. But it didn't seem likely. Unless they proved he'd been involved in framing Dave. Or unless something else happened.

The rest of the lunch period went by slowly. Sam was locking up the bin and Dave was slipping on his backpack when two girls, talking so intently they didn't even notice the boys, strolled by the booth.

"I just can't believe this election. First somebody starts an ugly rumor about Corky. Then we almost get a cheat for a president. And now we've got a thief," said one girl.

"Yeah. Imagine, stealing toys from needy kids. How scummy can you get?"

"Pretty scummy—if you're Brad Cohen."

Suddenly, both girls noticed Sam and Dave listening. One turned red. The other wrinkled her nose. "Come on, Lucy. There's a bad smell around here," she said, leading her friend away.

Neither Sam nor Dave said anything. They just stared at each other and slowly raised their eyebrows.

44

10

"All right, which one of you started it?" Brad's voice echoed off the metal doors of the locker room. All heads turned in his direction.

"Wait a minute, Brad," Jack said. "Don't blame them—"

"You shut up," Brad told him, and turned back to Sam and Dave. "Come on, which one of you?" he demanded, taking a threatening step toward them.

"Fight! Fight!" some of the other boys began to whisper excitedly.

Pulling on his sweat socks, Sam tensed up. He hated to fight, but he wasn't just going to stand there and get slugged.

Calmly, Dave said, "If you're talking about the rumor that you're a thief, we didn't start it."

"Come on, it's got to be either one of you or Mason and Lemon."

"It wasn't either of us," Dave repeated.

Brad continued to glare at them until Dan, whose locker was nearby, said something to him in a low voice. Then, slowly, he relaxed. "Ah, it doesn't matter anyway. You guys are too late. The

election's over. And I won it." Slamming his locker shut, Brad strode off toward the gym.

"Sorry about that," Dan said in his smooth voice. "But nobody likes to be accused of stealing." He followed Brad into the gym.

The crowd that had gathered in hope of seeing a fight moved away.

Dave turned to Jack. "Do you know who started this rumor?"

"I can guess," Jack said. "But I couldn't substantiate it."

"Is it Missy?"

"That would be my guess."

"Do you think the rumor's true? You said you were looking into the theft."

"Again, I have no proof, and as far as I know, Brad has no record of thievery."

"But?"

Jack waited a long moment before he said, "But he did have the opportunity. He was working at the booth the day the toys disappeared."

Suddenly, Mr. Gottlieb, the assistant gym teacher, boomed out, "Come on, guys. Move your sneakers. Class is starting."

Sam quickly laced up his hightops, while Dave locked his locker.

Jack was only half dressed. Sam and Dave left him scrambling into his shorts and walked into the gym.

"Missy's out to get Brad. Dan and/or Brad was out to get Corky. But who was out to get you?" Sam asked. "There are too many suspects and not enough clues."

"Maybe there are," said Dave, "and we're just not seeing them."

Sighing, they parted to join their squads.

11

Room 207 was packed tighter than Jack Dodge's father's briefcase. Kids who didn't even know what the Student Council did had turned up for the open meeting the new officers had called. They wanted to be there for whatever happened next in the dirtiest election their school had ever seen.

Sam and Dave were squashed against the wall at the back of the room, not far from Corky and Missy. Kids tossed nasty remarks their way. Sam wished he and Dave could go home, but he knew it was important for them to be there, not only to stick up for themselves, but because his funny feeling had returned. Something was going to happen at the meeting—and Bean Brothers, Private Eyes, had to be there when it did.

48

A few moments later, Brad arrived. He marched to the front of the room, surveyed the big crowd, and said, "Okay, everybody be quiet. We're going to talk about the candy sale. I've got some notes here. . . ." He reached for his backpack. But before he could open it, Jack interrupted quietly, "Mr. President?"

Brad looked at him irritably. "Yes, Mr. *Vice* President?"

"I believe it's customary to read the agenda and discuss old business first."

"The agenda is the candy sale." Brad brushed him off. "And as far as old business goes, nobody wants to hear that junk. Right?"

"Right!" some kids yelled back.

"Yeah, let's get to the candy sale," Lawson's voice boomed out.

Brad grinned and reached for his pack again.

"Mr. President?" said Karen Chen, the secretary. "How do you spell *agenda*?"

Brad rolled his eyes at her. "Ask the vice president. He seems to know everything. . . . Now, about the candy sale . . ."

For the third time, Brad grabbed at his pack. This time he managed to unzip it. He began to fumble inside for his notes. His eyes widened. He dropped the pack in horror. Out of it spilled a stuffed bear and a shiny Honka truck.

A gasp went up from the crowd. Sam and Dave gasped too.

"The toys! The toys from the Toy Drive!" Missy shouted.

"He *is* the thief," yelled Corky.

"I didn't . . . I couldn't have . . ." Brad stammered.

"Fire him!" "Impeach him!" "Make him quit!" cried different voices in the audience.

"But I didn't steal these. I didn't! They weren't even in my pack last period. Somebody must've—" He broke off, looked at Corky and Missy, then shook his head. "No, you couldn't have." Suddenly he spotted Sam and Dave across the room. "You! It was you!" He tried to charge at them, but there were too many people and desks in his path. He elbowed his way through. Dan and Jack tried to grab him, but he threw them off.

"Hold it, Brad," Dave called. "We didn't do it. Tell us when you last looked in your . . ." But his words were cut off by Lawson, who shoved him toward Brad.

"Cut it out!" Sam shouted at him.

"Make me," taunted Lawson, pushing Sam.

"Fight! Fight!" yelled some kids.

"Stop them!" yelled others.

Brad was near enough to Dave now to throw a punch. He did, but Dave ducked. "Listen, Brad . . ." He tried again. But Brad wasn't listening. Sam tried to pinion Brad's arms, but Lawson pushed him again.

51

Brad threw another punch. This one clipped Dave on the side of the head. "Owww," Dave said. His ear was ringing, and it hurt. He looked around wildly for an escape, but he was hemmed in on all sides by shouting kids.

"Leave him alone!" hollered Sam.

"Come on, chicken. You gonna fight me or not?" Lawson sneered.

"What's going on in here?" Dr. Barron's voice rang out. She waded into the room, parting the crowd and collaring Brad with one hand, Lawson with the other.

No one said anything at first. Then kids began to babble, "He . . . they . . . we . . ."

"Quiet! You, you, and you two . . ." Dr. Barron pointed to Brad, Lawson, and Sam and Dave. "Come along with me."

Rubbing his ear, Dave murmured to Sam, "I guess you might say this meeting is adjourned."

12

"At least Mom believes us about not starting the fight," Sam said, sitting up against the headboard of his bed. "Even if Dr. Barron didn't." He was trying to make his voice sound cheery—and he knew he wasn't succeeding. He felt terrible. The day had been awful. And the way things looked, the next day was going to be awful too.

Dave didn't respond. He'd been very quiet since Dr. Barron had warned them to shape up or else, and that troubled Sam. He was used to the two of them talking a lot, exchanging ideas. He watched Dave massage the side of his head. "Does it still hurt?" he asked.

"Hmmm?"

"Your ear. Does it still hurt?"

"Oh. Just a little."

Sam paused, wracking his brain for something hopeful to say, when Dave said, "If Brad's telling the truth, then neither Corky nor Missy could've done it."

It took Sam only a moment to figure out what Dave meant. "You mean about the toys not being in his pack before gym?" he asked.

"Yes. Corky and Missy couldn't have slipped them into his pack, because they couldn't have gotten into the boys' locker room. That's why he accused us."

"Right. That's if Brad's telling the truth—which I doubt."

"You do? I can think of a lot of things Brad Cohen might be, but a thief? I don't know. . . ."

"If he had anything to do with stuffing the ballot box, he could just as well be a thief, too," Sam pointed out.

They were both silent for a moment. Then Sam said, "Okay, let's say Brad is innocent. If he didn't put the toys in his pack and Corky and Missy couldn't have, who did? Who'd want to get Brad in trouble?"

"The same person who wanted to get me and Corky in trouble. The same person who stuffed the ballot box and started the rumor about her."

Sam ticked off suspects in his head. "Dan!" he yelled excitedly. "Dan is the only one left who could've done all three things." Then he frowned. "Why would Dan want to frame Brad? They're friends."

"I know. It doesn't make sense," said Dave. "And I can't make it make sense."

They stopped talking again and heard the phone ringing distantly, followed a few moments later by footsteps outside their door and their mother's voice calling, "Sam, Dave, Rita's mother's on the phone."

"Rita's mother?" Puzzled, they hurried out of their room.

Dave took the receiver. "Oh hello, Ms. O'Toole. How's Rita? Oh, I'm glad to hear that. Yes . . . Yes . . . All right . . . Thank you." He hung up.

Sam burst out, "What is it? What did she want? How's Rita? Is she . . ."

"Rita's better, but she's very hoarse. She just heard about the election and she told her mother to call and ask us to come over. She's got something to show us."

"What is it?"

"Ms. O'Toole didn't say."

"When? When are we going?"

"How about right now?" said Dave.

"I can't let you boys go up to Rita's room. She may still be contagious," Ms. O'Toole told Sam and Dave as she ushered them into the living room. "I'm busy with a report, so Leroy will act as a go-between."

"Leroy?" said Sam.

"That's my name. Don't wear it out," Rita's younger brother razzed as he entered the room.

Sam and Dave turned to him and sighed. They knew Leroy quite well from the time they'd all gotten mixed up with the Killerdiller Gang. He'd been a pest then. And he hadn't changed one bit.

"Well, I'll leave you to take care of your business," said Ms. O'Toole. She left the room.

"Okay, how much are you going to give me?"

"Give you? For what?" asked Dave.

"For being a messenger. Rita gave me a quarter. But that was just for carrying the goods. Delivering them's a different story. It's worth more. So how much are you going to give me?"

"I'll give you a—" Sam began.

But Dave cut him off. "Just what are 'the goods'?"

Slowly, Leroy dug into his back pocket, pulled out a piece of paper, and dangled it in front of them. "This. Rita says she thinks it's important. She says it might help you figure out who fixed the election."

"What!" Sam yelled and made a grab for the paper.

But Leroy snatched it back and danced out of reach.

"Leroy," Dave said calmly. "Give me the goods."

"Give me the money."

"I don't have any."

"What about him?" Leroy nodded at Sam.

"He doesn't either."

"Then forget it."

"Okay," said Dave. "But it's too bad I can't forget that I saw you trying to 'borrow' Ozzie Ripkin's skateboard last week without his permission."

Leroy's freckled face turned pale. "Hey, you're not going to tell Ozzie about that, are you?"

"Not if you give me the paper."

"Here." Leroy practically threw it at him, but it was Sam who caught and unfolded it. Dave went over to him and peered over his shoulder. Leroy sidled over for a peek.

Both of them inhaled sharply.

"Your signature," Sam said. "Someone was practicing it . . ."

". . . to forge the ballots and stuff the box with them," Dave finished.

They stared down at the stationery for so long that Leroy couldn't stand it. "So, who did it?" he blurted out. Dave ignored him and pointed to the torn corner. "What do you think this means, Sam?" he asked.

Sam read the letters aloud, " 'esk of/ge, Esq. . . .' 'esk of,' 'esk of.' I've seen that before on . . . on . . . 'Desk of!' 'From the desk of!' Dad's got a memo pad that says that. I bet that's what this one says too."

"Hey, yeah!" Leroy yelled. "My mom has one of those too!"

"I think you're right," said Dave. "But what about this part—'ge, Esq.'? 'Esq.' looks like some kind of abbreviation. But I don't know what it means."

"Rita probably does," said Leroy.

"Does what?" a raspy voice said.

The three boys looked up. Standing at the top of the staircase, her hair messy and her nose red, was Rita.

"Rita, you should be in bed," Sam said, concerned and a little embarrassed at seeing her in her bathrobe and slippers.

"Yeah, Mom's gonna kill you," Leroy told her.

"It's just for a minute. I'm not coming downstairs. But you were taking so long to come, Leroy, I had to get up. . . . So, is the paper important?"

"You bet it is," said Dave. "It tells us who fixed the election—if you can tell us what 'Esq.' means."

"It's an abbreviation for esquire," Rita said promptly.

"Esquire?"

"Yes. It originally meant 'squire to a knight.' But now—and I just looked this up—it's used as a polite title for lawyers. You'd address a letter to Leo Lawyer, Esquire."

"Lawyers," said Dave. He looked at Sam.

" 'From the desk of blank-ge, Esquire,' " Sam was muttering. " 'From the desk of blank-ge, lawyer.' " Suddenly, he stopped. His eyes widened. He stared back at Dave. "No, it couldn't be."

"Yes, it could," Dave said slowly, as the truth hit him too. "It all fits."

"What does?" "Who did it?" said Rita and Leroy simultaneously.

"He's the only one with opportunity, ability, and most important, motive," Dave went on. "He's the only one who could have wanted to disqualify Corky, Brad, and me. It has to be him."

"Who?" Rita and Leroy yelled again.

Dave turned to them. "Jack Dodge," he said.

13

❧

"As you all heard earlier today, Brad Cohen has resigned as president of the Student Council. If a president resigns, the vice president succeeds him. I was your vice president. Now I'm your president," Jack addressed the second open meeting of the Student Council held within a week.

"Hey, this school's going to make the *Guinness Book of Records* for the most Student Council presidents in the shortest amount of time," a girl called out.

Kids giggled.

"Quiet, please," said Jack. "We'll begin this meeting with . . ." He began to read the agenda.

Out in the hall, Dave whispered to Sam, Brad, Dan, Corky, and Missy, "Okay, ready?"

"Ready," they said.

"And now, our first order of business . . ." Jack went on.

"Set?"

"Set."

"Last year, the Council decided to . . ."

"Go!"

"Go!"

In a single file, Dave, Sam, and company marched

into room 207 and formed a line directly in front of Jack.

"The playground should be . . ."

"Look! Look who's here!" "Hey, what's going on?" "What are they doing? I thought they hated each other . . ." kids muttered.

Jack looked up and blinked. His mouth twitched nervously. But in his most formal voice, he said, "Hello, Sam, Dave, Brad, Dan, Corky, and Missy. Glad you could all make the meeting. Please, uh, take your seats. The meeting's already in progress . . ."

Missy cut him off. "Jack Dodge, you are on trial."

"The charges," announced Dan, glancing down at a slip of paper, "are defamation of character, theft, forgery, election fraud, and skullduggery. Are you prepared to hear the evidence against you?"

"What?" "Huh?" "What's going on?" demanded the audience.

Jack raised his voice above the din. "Evidence? This—this isn't a courtroom. This is, uh, a Student Council meeting. And you are all out of order."

"Tell that to the judge," said Missy. She nodded to the doorway, which Lawson, along with three of his fellow football players, was now blocking.

Jack opened his mouth to say something else, but nothing came out.

It was Corky's turn to speak. "Exhibit A—a signed affidavit from Ms. Gardella, receptionist at Spudnuts, Inc., stating that a boy with a *nasal voice*, calling himself Dave Bean, phoned and asked if Corky Lemon was related to the owner of the company. Ms. Gardella told the boy that Corky is the owner's niece and that her uncle offered her a commission on Spudnuts sold in this school." Corky turned to Dave. "Did you make that call?"

"I did not," he replied.

"I believe you," said Corky. "Oh, yes . . ." She turned to face the other kids in the room. "For the record, Corky Lemon *turned down* her uncle's offer—and here's an affidavit from him, swearing to that."

Corky moved back into line and Brad stepped out. "Brad Cohen stated at the previous open meeting of the Student Council that the toys, missing since that morning, which fell out of his pack were not there before the previous period, which was gym. Who had access to these toys besides him? Missy Mason and Judy Lupner. Could either of them have slipped the toys into his pack during gym? No. Only a guy could have—a guy who was in Brad's gym class, who dawdled in the locker room, showing up last in his squad. A guy who had easy access to the toys all day long—because he himself set up the booth and could get the key from Ms. Lutz anytime he wanted to. Can you guess who that guy is?"

Jack swallowed hard.

Brad gave him a vicious grin, then motioned to Dave. "Your turn."

"Last week, Dave Bean signed a 'Save the Trees' petition. He doesn't have a copy of said petition. But he does have this—Exhibit C." Dave opened his hands, dropping a bunch of the forged ballots on Jack's desk. "And this—Exhibit D." He laid the ripped piece of stationery Rita had found on top of the ballots. "I don't yet have Exhibit E, an unmarked, untorn piece of this stationery, but it'll be easy enough to get when—and if—we stop by your father's office after this meeting, Jack."

"No! No, don't do that. *Please* don't do that," Jack, trembling, shouted. "I'll confess! I'll confess! I started the rumor about Corky. I took the toys and put them in Brad's pack in the locker room. I forged Dave's signature and stuffed the ballot box. I sneaked back into Dr. Barron's office after Sam—and then Corky—left and before Ms. Lutz returned."

"But why?" someone asked.

Jack's lips quivered. "I've . . . I've always wanted to be Student Council president. Ever since first grade. But . . . but people don't like me very much, and I knew they'd never vote for me. This year when nobody else decided to run for vice president, I saw a way to become president . . . whether or not I got the votes." He paused and swallowed. "I . . . I know it was wrong. And I deserve to be punished for it. I hereby resign as vice president and from all my other activities, and I throw myself on the mercy of the court."

"Judge?" Missy looked at Lawson. "What do you recommend?"

Lawson sliced a finger across his throat.

Jack sank his head into his hands.

"All right," said Missy. "Take him away to Dr. Barron."

"May it please the court," Sam spoke up quietly. "I think we should show a little mercy. I think we should accept Jack's resignation as vice president, but let him keep running the Toy Drive, the Save the Trees committee, the Pets for Peace campaign, and his other activities."

"Judge?" Missy turned to Lawson again.

"Sure," he said. "Why not? Nobody else wants to do that stuff anyway. Now let's take a walk to Dr. Barron's office, Dodge."

It was a long moment before Jack rose. He walked silently toward the door, but when he passed Sam and Dave he smiled, weakly.

Sam nodded at him.

"Well," Dave said, after he and Lawson were gone. "I guess we'd better join them and find out when we all get to vote again."

"Right," said Sam.

"Right," Dan and Missy repeated. They looked at their candidates.

But Brad and Corky weren't looking at them. They were glaring at each other.

"You'll never win this time," Corky said.

"Ha, Spudnutter. That's what you think," hissed Brad.

"Here we go again," Sam said.

"Here we go again," echoed Dave.

14

"Congratulations, Dave." "Way to go." "Good luck, Old Bean."

Dave smiled and said thanks to the kids saluting him as he and Sam walked down the hall. He'd done it. He'd won, fair and square. And this time everybody knew it.

"Boy, am I glad our name's not *mud* anymore," he said to Sam.

"Yeah," Sam agreed. "It's bad enough being stuck with *Bean*." Then, more seriously, he said, "I think everybody's really glad you won."

Before Dave could say anything, Corky and Missy appeared. They took one look at Sam and Dave, harrumphed, and walked by with their noses in the air. Just after they turned the corner, Brad and Dan appeared. Brad spotted the Bean Brothers and scowled. Dan didn't even look their way.

"Well, almost everybody," Sam amended.

They neared the Toy Drive booth. Jack was running it. He bobbed his head at them, but he looked embarrassed and more than a little sad.

"You know, it's funny. What he did was pretty bad, and I guess I should be mad at him, but somehow I can't help feeling sorry for the guy."

"Yeah. I know what you mean," Sam agreed. Jack was going to have to live with what he'd done, and Sam didn't think he was going to find it easy.

They passed the booth and moved on to the exit. "Well," Dave said, "I think it's time to have that celebration. How does that kitchen sink pizza sound to you now?"

"Great!" Sam said, then frowned.

"What's wrong?"

"Nothing—it's just that Rita still can't celebrate with us."

"Sure she can," said Dave.

"What do you mean? She's not in school. She can't go to Roma's."

"Right, but there's no reason Roma's can't come to her."

"Huh?"

"I called her house. Her mother said she's definitely not contagious anymore. In fact, she's

67

coming back to school tomorrow. So Ms. O'Toole's invited us over there—with the pizza."

"Great!"

"There's only one catch. . . ." Dave paused.

"Uh-oh," said Sam.

"Yup. Leroy. He's going to celebrate with us." Sam groaned.

"Think of it this way." Dave patted his brother's shoulder. "It could be a lot worse."

"How?"

"Leroy could be twins."